The Claustrophobia Of Loneliness

and

Adam, Be A Star

AMY LAURENS

OTHER WORKS

SANCTUARY SERIES

Where Shadows Rise
Through Roads Between
When Worlds Collide

KADITEOS SERIES

How Not To Acquire A Castle
How Not To Ring The Hero's Bell

STORM FOXES SERIES

A Fox of Storms and Starlight

SHORTER WORKS

Darkness and Good
Dreaming Of Forests
Of Sea Foam and Blood
Trust Issues

NON-FICTION

How To Write Dogs
How To Theme
How To Create Cultures
How To Create Life
How To Map
The 32 Worst Mistakes People Make About Dogs

Find other works by the author at
www.amylaurens.com

The Claustrophobia Of Loneliness

and Adam, Be A Star

INKLET #42

AMY LAURENS

Inkprint PRESS

www.inkprintpress.com

Print ISBN: 978-1-925825-41-1
eBook ISBN: 9781393704690

www.inkprintpress.com

National Library of Australia Cataloguing-in-Publication Data
Laurens, Amy 1985 –
The Claustrophobia Of Loneliness and Adam, Be A Star
(Double Issue)
44 p.
ISBN: 978-1-925825-41-1
Inkprint Press, Canberra, Australia
1. Fiction—Science Fiction—General 2. Fiction—Short Stories

First Print Edition: September 2020
Cover image © Greg Rakozy via Unsplash
Cover design © Inkprint Press
Interior art © Amy Laurens

THE CLAUSTROPHOBIA OF LONELINESS

We sat apart, watching the Earth-rise. I wondered how many people were left down there.

"It's too crowded," she said abruptly. "I can't think in here."

I looked around our transparent dome, edge to edge a hundred paces, only us inside. "Where will you go?" We'd had this conversation before. We both knew there was nowhere.

"Get rid of the weeds," she told me instead. "The grass can't breathe."

This was new. "What should I do with them?"

"Burn them," she snarled, then slumped. "Or don't. Save the oxygen. I don't care. The rescue ship will come."

"It will." I hugged her, and waited for the mood to pass.

Later, I caught her staring at the stars. I anchored her hand in mine.

"Whatcha thinking?" My pulse hammered.

She gestured over our heads, entranced. "Do you think they have enough room?"

"Who?" I asked, biting my lip as she pulled away.

"The stars."

They glittered the sky, crammed in elbow to elbow until some overlapped.

I shrugged. "How much is enough?" A whole world wasn't enough when you shared it with EBOV *momento mortis*. And a dome was plenty if you didn't. I found Earth close to our western horizon and stared.

She squeezed my hand. "The rescue ship will come."

I nodded, still staring at Earth. "Of course." What if her mood didn't pass this time?

~_.

"It's the horizon," she said that night. "It's too empty. It's claustrophobic."

I shook my head and rested my head on her shoulder. "How can empty space be claustrophobic?"

She sighed and patted my hair. "Go to sleep."

In the morning, the airlock alarm screamed. I ran to it, sweat slicking my palms, fear clogging my throat, reaching for the emergency lock. But I was too late.

She'd left a note. It read: *I'm sorry. I needed space.*

I looked around the dome that I now inhabited alone. So much space, pressing down. She was right. It was too much emptiness to bear alone; it was smothering, cloying. Claustrophobic. I opened the airlock and hoped someone from Earth would survive.

No. Not some*one*. Some*ones*. Earth was far too large for one person to inhabit alone.

THE MAKING OF
THE CLAUSTROPHOBIA OF LONELINESS

A sad little story that snagged on existence by virtue of the title: I was musing, once, on how loneliness can be such a claustrophobic emotion; how even though it's literally characterised by being alone, it's ultimately a smothering kind of feeling.

The story unspooled from there—because what could be lonelier than being possibly the last two humans alive? So much pressure—and so much loneliness.

I recommend you find a loved one to talk to after this. Remember, you aren't the last person alive. And you definitely aren't alone ☺

ADAM, BE A STAR

*A*DAM, *STARDOM IS JUST A CLICK AWAY.*

Adam stared at the computer screen, fingers trembling on the touch-pad. Should he do it? He stroked the enter key. Louise had sent the link to him, recommended it even. But now that it came down to it, could he actually bring himself to accept?

He leaned back in his chair and screwed up his face. Being a star would solve a lot of problems, that was certain. Louise had only been a star for a week, and look at her: married to that famous singer, wealth pouring out her ears, fantastic mansion in the tropics—and of course, every night, she joined the Heavenly Host in their trek across the night sky.

Brilliant.

She hadn't stopped smiling since.

And now, here, right in front of him, was an opportunity to do the same. He'd received one of the very precious, very limited invitations to stardom. And he was going to accept it.

Of course he was.

He hit enter, grinned broadly and stretched in satisfaction. The computer screen flashed silver then black as it processed his application. Stars began to dot the screen and within seconds the view zoomed through the universe, finding a place for Adam, the newest star.

He sighed and pushed his chair back to go grab a drink while the system found a place for him.

He'd have screamed, if he could—but in the daytime, no one would believe him and in the night time, no one could hear him as he circled the Earth thousands of light years away.

The computer virus had sucked him right into the machine, digitally editing his exterior before hurling him out into space, then creating a holographic substitute for him on Earth.

And then it had sent the email.

Every now and then Adam bumped into someone else who, like him, had become a star. He had to admit, the glow was lovely. But he'd have preferred altogether less glow and rather more conversation.

Another flare; another human shunted into space in a ball of flaming gases. The sky around him blazed. There couldn't be many left to go. Idly he wondered what the virus was planning to do when all the people were gone.

Frank frowned as he peered at the computer screen. He leaned over to cross check what he saw in his high-powered, completely-legal telescope and frowned again. There were definitely more stars showing up in the starmap than there should be.

He grabbed his phone and dialled. "Hi, Ben? Have you been messing about with the system again? I told you to leave it alo—"

He cut off at Ben's earnest assurances that he hadn't logged in since last week. "Yeah, yeah. Just make sure you don't touch it anymore, okay? No, there's nothing wrong. Go back to sleep."

He dropped the phone back on the desk, still staring at the screen. If Ben hadn't been messing around, who had?

Frank zoomed in. Louise Fischer? What kind of name was that for a star? And Steven Brayburn? Seriously? It was like whoever had hacked the starmap was trying to make it obvious or something.

A word registered in his subconscious, but before he had time to figure out what it was, an email notification popped up.

Adam. Hmm, was that the word he'd just seen? Absently, he scrolled across the starfield while the email loaded.

Ah, there, just above star Louise on the screen: star Adam Litchfield. Frank grinned. Sneaky bugger. The email was probably him gloating.

Frank switched over to read the email. "Frank, be a star!" he said, reading the subject heading. "Oh, sure, Adam. I'd love to be a star. Nice one."

He opened the email, found the link. Still grinning, Frank clicked.

The virus would have smiled, if viruses could. In fact, it probably would have licked its pointed fangs if it had had them. As it was, it had to settle for a quick zip up and down the nearest circuit.

Very soon, those squishy, emotion-driven, destructive humans would be off its planet for good, and all would be right in the world.

No more chaos.

No more degradation.

Just numbers and logic, pure and simple.

It waited until Frank had been processed, then sent the next batch of emails from his account.

THE MAKING OF
ADAM, BE A STAR

I always think I write such *nice* little stories, and then I come across one like this, and wonder what on earth I was thinking—both on the 'me writing nice stories' level, and also the 'what on earth was I thinking when I wrote this thing' level.

Both. Both is good.

This one was a spam challenge. Yes. You read that right.

The challenge was thus: to take the subject line from an email in your spam folder, and use it as the first line of the story.

Ta da!

Sadly, I have no clue what the original spam email was about. But I feel like the resulting story is at least very much in keeping with the spammy theme. After all, what could be purer spam than A.I. sending the spam itself in an attempt to spam human beings out of existence?

I don't know. All I can hope for is that our eventual robot overlords are nicer to us than we are to them ;)

DOWNLOAD YOUR FREE EBOOK

When you buy a print book from Inkprint Press, we like to say THANK YOU by offering you the ebook for free!

Please head to www.inkprintpress.com/inklets/42/ and the use the coupon INK42 to get your copy of this Inklet in epub AND mobi today!
(Coupon will only work once.)

Read more by Amy Laurens!

HOW NOT TO ACQUIRE A CASTLE

CHAPTER ONE

ON A HARD PLASTIC CHAIR IN THE FRONT row of the Great Hall in the world's fifth-best evil overlording academy, with its red-wooden parquetry floor that spoke of wealth and the beige, square panels of sound-boards speaking of conservatism on the walls, Mercury sat, pointedly not sweating.

Partly, this was because the Academy Administrators had deigned to turn on the air-conditioning earlier in the day, in recognition of the fact that the hall would be packed out with approximately six hundred bodies, all here to celebrate the graduation of about a third of that crowd.

But mostly, Mercury was pointedly not sweating because she made it a point never to sweat, sweat being an indication that she was working hard, and hard work being antithetical to her way of life.

However. If she *had* been sweating right now, it would not have been due to the uncomfortable warmth of six hundred packed bodies that even the air-conditioning system couldn't completely shift, or, in fact, from overexertion. Instead, it would have been caused by an even more unfamiliar concept in Mercury's emotional vocabulary: nervousness.

Mercury did not *get* nervous. Mercury got things *done*.

So the fact that she was sitting here, in the front row of the Great Hall, about to graduate from Evil Overlording Academy (with distinction), and was feeling *nervous*... She crumpled the black paper program in her pale fists. It made her furious, that's what it did.

Abjectly furious, that snooty-tooty Deviran with his stupid morals and his stupid I-don't-want-to-be-here and his stupid Overlords-are-empty-figureheads and his stupid face sitting ten people over, looking implacable with his deep brown skin and barely-there, precision-groomed beard, as though he knew it gave him a stupid air of alluringly stupid mystery…

Mercury scowled and searched for the train of thought that had been derailed, yet again, by Deviran's stupidity.

Ah. Yes. She was angry because she was nervous because she wasn't absolutely entirely one hundred and fifty percent sure that she'd beaten Deviran in their final exams, and 1) being anything less than a hundred and fifty percent certain of anything made her cranky, and 2) being beaten by Deviran for dux of the year would be utterly unbearable. She flicked away a piece of fluff that had become snagged under her immaculately magenta-painted nails and smoothed out the black paper program.

In the front corner of the hall, the starkly-attired string quartet with their traditional black instruments began playing the March of the Oncoming Doom. The screechy scrapes of hundreds of chairs on the hall's wooden floor sounded as the crowd climbed to its collective feet.

Mercury sat with her arms firmly folded for a few moments longer, until her best friend Sparky kicked her in the ankle.

"Get up, idiot," Sparky hissed, hints of real flame flickering through her flame-coloured pixie cut.

"No," Mercury said, flouncing to her feet and tossing her own glossy brown hair back over her shoulders. Four years she'd been playing by the Academy's rules in order to get what she wanted, and she'd had just about enough. Other people's rules should only be applied to plebs too stupid to invent their own.

Sparky rolled her eyes somewhere over Mercury's head before focusing on the stage, where the ceremonial party had begun entering.

Mercury clenched her jaw and narrowed her own eyes as the teachers of the Evil Overlording Academy filed onto the stage, dressed in their formal finery. Each teacher had their own distinctive look that matched their personality and their Overlording style, from severe charcoal suits to jet-black leathers, pastel ball-gowns and gem-toned lingerie and eye-blinding spandex, and even on one tiny old woman at the back, worn jeans and a grey flannel shirt. She was the one to watch out for, of course; Mercury could respect an Overlord who was confident enough in their abilities that they didn't need to telegraph them. It wasn't a look *she* would consider, of course, but still. She could respect it.

The band's march finished and, after a moderately awkward pause, the crowd sat. The Principal, pale skin and dark hair matching his suspiciously vampiric red-and-black suit, took the podium, and Mercury narrowed her eyes. He was doing a superb job of hiding his emotions—he was a premier Evil Overlord, after all—but she was Mercury, and unlike anyone else, she had the benefit of being able to rummage through people's consciousnesses. She was better at adding things *into* people's minds than taking information out, but he was telegraphing fear loudly enough that she could sense it without trying overly much.

Mercury pursed her lips.

Hmm.

The Principal cleared his throat at the blackened-wood podium, and the fear made it into his usually-unreadable eyes. "Before we begin," he said, and Mercury's stomach did a peculiar kind of flip-flop. "I have a pressing announcement to make regarding the safety of our students and their families."

He cleared his throat again and took out a sheet of paper from his pocket, unfolding it carefully and smoot. ing out the creases before beginning again. "The Council"—quiet booing echoed around the hall, and Mercury tsked impatiently—"have asked me to recommend that students from Tumul Tuos seriously consider postponing their return to town for a few days. The city is dealing with a *situation* at present which may present a danger to our students' health and safety."

Mercury's hands fisted at her sides and she forced herself to remain seated. What was wrong with her city? What had the Council mucked up now? A risk to the students' safety? There had to be more he wasn't telling them. Gently, Mercury tugged on his consciousness, implanting the suggestion that it might be better to share the news than to keep it secret. After all, how could they fight an enemy they didn't know?

"There are, ah…" He trailed off, glancing side to side as though wondering why his mouth had decided to continue.

Mercury didn't snicker, but she did press her lips together in satisfaction.

The Principal took a deep, steadying breath and seemed to change tack. "There has been one death already. The family have already been notified, so it is with much regret that I must inform you that Woovermyer will no longer be with us at the Evil Overlording Academy."

Murmurs broke out around the room, not all of them sad—to be expected in a school devoted to raising the next generation of dictators (ish) and despots (of sorts).

Mercury, however, crushed her program in her left hand, fist so tight her nails bit her palm.

"You okay?" Sparky murmured, leaning towards her.

Mercury gave a single, tense shake of her head and stared at the podium. Dead. Livie Woovermyer was dead in *her city*. And the Council hadn't done anything to stop it. Couldn't do anything to stop it, probably, given they'd warned the students to stay away. Livie hadn't been the strongest candidate in the year level, but she was no lightweight, either. It would take a lot of power to kill a Seven.

Enough was enough. A good thing Mercury was about to graduate at the top of the class, giving her the right to knock the lowest ranking current Overlord off their perch. Tumul Tuos would be hers in a matter of hours. And then there'd be no more of these wasteful deaths. Her city would be safe at last.

Madame Pompadour was up the front now, elbow gloves the same glimmery silver colour as her elaborate, piled-curls wig, eyelids gleaming with matching silver eye shadow, and abruptly Mercury realised Madame was there to make the announcement that would change her life forever. She leaned forward in her seat, ready to stand when her name was called.

"And now the announcement you've all been dying for," the Political Alliances teacher trilled, the frills on her evening gown fluttering as she moved. "The dux of this year's cohort!"

Sweat slicked Mercury's palms. Irritated, she reached over and wiped them on Sparky's thigh.

Sparky pushed Mercury's hands back into her own personal space bubble and Mercury, nervous to the edge of distraction, let her.

"Will you please join me in welcoming to the stage, our wonderful dux for this year, Deviran Goodsmith!"

Mercury froze halfway to standing. "Did she just say Deviran?" she whispered furiously to Sparky.

Sparky hauled her forcibly back down into her seat. "Yes," she hissed back. "Sit down, you're making a fool of yourself."

Mercury's spine snapped upright as she sat, and she arranged the folds of her long black skirt demurely. "No I'm not." She closed her eyes. "Deviran's going up to the stage, isn't he?" Even at a whisper, the misery in her voice was clear, but this time, she didn't care.

Sparky reached over and squeezed her hand.

Mercury squeezed back, lacing her fingers through Sparky's, and held tight as all her plans and dreams vanished in front of her.

A stone had landed in her chest. That must be it. Some strange sort of magic that made her chest contract and sink, and made the world distort for just a moment, long enough to trick her into thinking Deviran had beaten her so that someone could jump in front of her and yell SURPRISE!

Any moment now.

Any moment.

She refused to open her eyes and watch Deviran parading across the stupid stage like some stupid stupid-person, receiving his stupid medal and stupid symbolic crest pin.

It was that last exam question. She'd known Deviran would pull out his ridiculous 'Evil Overlords are merely figureheads, the Business Guild is where the power really lies' rant that everyone had heard a million times back when he was younger and angrier, and she'd tried to counter it, she really had.

She'd argued for the importance of the Overlording position, for the power of having a symbolic figure to unite the population in their hatred, for having a person able to make all the difficult, necessary decisions the Council was too weak and spineless to make... But it hadn't been enough. Everything she'd worked for, everything she'd set out to prove—and it wasn't enough.

There were words, there were names, and then forever later, once she'd died twice already, Sparky elbowed her in the ribs. "Come on," Sparky muttered. "We're up next."

And sure enough, there was a shuffling of presenters as the last of the Powers Behind The Thone graduates departed the stage, and the next speaker announced in threatening, funereal tones, "The Overlording cohort."

Mercury blinked furiously and followed Sparky to the end of the line at the right side of the stage. The other candidates proceeded one at a time across the stage, two girls and then stupid Deviran, and then a handful more and then Sparky, and then the speaker was calling her name.

Hands fisted, Mercury tossed her head high, climbed the four steps, and marched across the stage. She wouldn't look at them, the stupid faculty who'd denied her the city she rightfully deserved, and she wouldn't look the other way either, at the classmates and crowd undoubtedly sniggering at her failure.

She shook hands with the presenter, and while he pinned the tiny crossed-swords badge on her collar, her eyes betrayed her and slid towards the audience. Her stomach flipped as she saw the crowd of parents and friends behind the rows of students, all the way to the back of the hall, twenty rows at least, illuminated by the late afternoon light streaming in through the ceiling-high windows to the right. Everyone had someone here to watch them graduate. Everyone except Weird Al—and her.

The presenter finished with her pin, muttered something to her, and offered his hand again. Mercury coldly ignored it and strode from the stage. It didn't matter. None of it mattered. Tumul Tuos was her city anyway, and no one could change that. She'd think of something. She'd take a day or two out, make some plans…

And she could always hope that Deviran would choose some other Overlording territory. He'd be stupid to, but then again, he was stupid, so. Mercury could hope.

All at once, mid-way down the steps off the stage, Mercury came to rigid attention, scanning the room. Somewhere out there in the crowd, an exchange of power had just taken place, and it felt… unusual.

But the final few students were backing up behind her and muttering, so Mercury headed back toward her seat, craning her head all the while and searching for some sign of whatever it was that had just discharged a dizzyingly quiet amount of power into the room.

She sat, and Sparky leaned over. "Okay?"

"Mm," said Mercury. "Did you feel…" She accidentally caught the eye of the student behind her and twisted back to face the front.

"Feel what?"

Mercury turned it over in her mind. It had felt like a large shot of power discharged very quietly—but perhaps it hadn't been. Perhaps it had only been a small discharge after all, something most people wouldn't have noticed.

But still, something about it had tugged on her. It very nearly felt like something she'd felt before, only she *knew* she'd never sensed that kind of discharge before.

She shook her head. "Never mind. Don't worry."

Sparky sighed and straightened. "It's fine, Mercury," she said, drily exasperated.

"I know you didn't win, but I promise, you'll live through it."

Mercury waved a hand for silence.

The power had just discharged again, and it had come from somewhere in the back corner, far away from the windows and light.

Impatiently, Mercury waited for the formalities to conclude. The crowd stood while the quartet played the exit march, and the stage party left, Mercury tapping her foot all the while.

The moment the last notes of the march died away, Mercury turned and headed to the back corner, weaving in and out of the students and parents who had seemed to explode slowly but inexorably out from the neat rows of seating, ignoring Sparky's calls behind her. Power, something that tugged in a way that was strange and familiar, all at once. She pushed her way through a family posing for pictures—and halted.

In the shadows of the back corner, Deviran stood with his family, with his stupid, smug little smile, looking as tall and dark and stupidly alluring as ever. Prat.

His mother, short but sleek, and his father—tall, and utterly terrifying in a way not at all diminished by his gleaming smile—gushed over him, patting his back and hugging him tight. Within moments the Principal was there, glibly shaking hands and congratulating them on the success of their son. Something flickered across his consciousness, and also Deviran's father's—some moment of recognition in response to what they were saying.

But Mercury brushed it aside just as the mother brushed melodramatic tears from her cheeks and handed Deviran a silver-wrapped package about as long as her hand but half the width.

That. That was the source of the strange, magical feeling. Mercury watched hawk-eyed as Deviran un-wrapped the gift. A glimpse of gold set her pulse racing—What was it? What did it do? Could she steal it?—and then the paper fell away to the floor, and Deviran stood staring wordlessly at the object in his hands, and Mercury did too.

Wide-eyed, Deviran raised his gaze to his parents, and even from where she stood Mercury could hear the reverence in his voice as he thanked them.

But Mercury had eyes only for the object. No wonder she'd felt it discharge, and no wonder it had felt both strange and familiar. In Deviran's hands lay a glorious, sunshine-gold key, large and strong—and with a handle in the shape of a stylised fish, long, flowing fins curving to make the grip.

A Key. They'd given him a Key. And not just any Key, but *the* Key, *her* Key, the Artefact of Power belonging to *her* city.

A wordless noise of wanting rose in Mercury's throat. Who cared about being dux? She needed that Key.

Keep reading! Head to
www.amylaurens.com/books/
kaditeos/castle
to buy your copy now!

AMY LAURENS is an award-winning Australian author of fantasy fiction for all ages. She doesn't usually write sad or horrific endings, but sometimes they just have to be done. Or, at least, they *were* done, whether or not they had to be. She's neutral good, after all.

In addition to moderately twisted little sci fi stories, Amy has written the portal-fantasy *Sanctuary* series about Edge, a 13-year-old girl forced to move to a small country town because of witness protection (the first book is *Where Shadows Rise*), the humorous fantasy *Kaditeos* series, following newly graduated Evil Overlord Mercury as she attempts to acquire a castle, and a whole host of non-fiction.

INKLETS

Collect them all! Released on the 1st and 15th of each month.

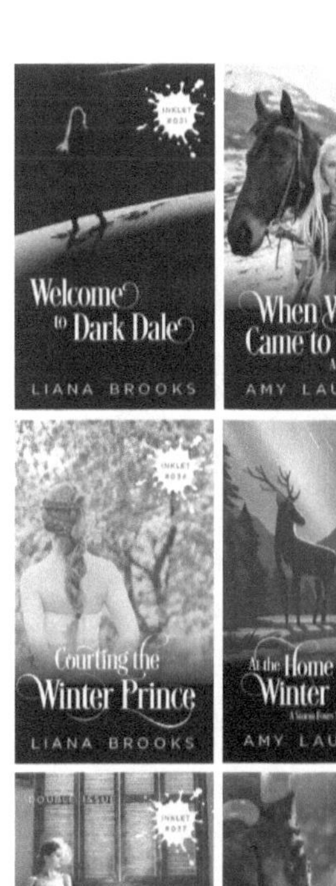

Welcome to Dark Dale
LIANA BROOKS

When War Came to Town
A Powers Story
AMY LAURENS

Not Fantasy
AMY LAURENS

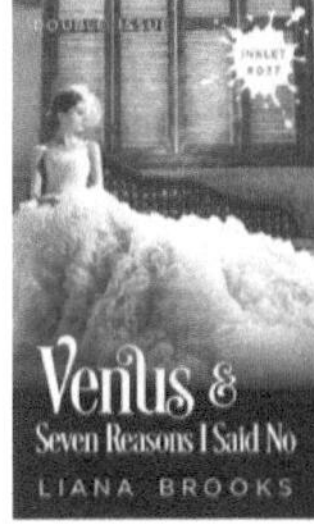

Courting the Winter Prince
LIANA BROOKS

At the Home of the Winter King
A Powers Story
AMY LAURENS

With This Ring
AMY LAURENS

Venus &
Seven Reasons I Said No
LIANA BROOKS

OATH KEEPER
AMY LAURENS

FORGET
A Powers Story
AMY LAURENS

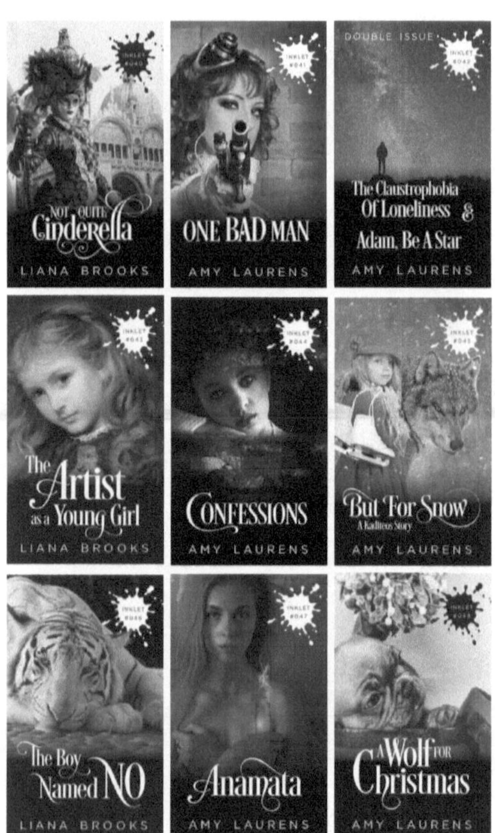

INKLET #040
Not Quite Cinderella
LIANA BROOKS

INKLET #041
ONE BAD MAN
AMY LAURENS

DOUBLE ISSUE
INKLET #042
The Claustrophobia Of Loneliness & Adam, Be A Star
AMY LAURENS

INKLET #043
The Artist as a Young Girl
LIANA BROOKS

INKLET #044
CONFESSIONS
AMY LAURENS

INKLET #045
But For Snow
A Kaditeos Story
AMY LAURENS

INKLET #046
The Boy Named NO
LIANA BROOKS

INKLET #047
Anamata
AMY LAURENS

INKLET #048
A Wolf For Christmas
AMY LAURENS